Breaking, Healing, Conquering

DELETED DRAFTS

Written by
SARYA JOHAR

BlueRose ONE .com
Stories Matter
NewDelhi • London

BLUEROSE PUBLISHERS
India | U.K.

BlueRose ONE.com
Stories Matter
New Delhi • London

For permissions requests or inquiries regarding this publication, please contact:

BLUEROSE PUBLISHERS
www.BlueRoseONE.com
info@bluerosepublishers.com
+91 8882 898 898
+4407342408967

ISBN: 978-93-7310-227-6

Cover design: Daksh
Typesetting: Tanya Raj Upadhyay

First Edition: November 2025

when summer feels the pain,
it gives way to rain

TABLE OF CONTENTS

SCARS

They are here to stay
Even when the memories fade away
A few years down the line
They tone down and don't shine
Still can be seen with an eye curious to look
And heard by ears wanting to know the real me like I'm the most beautiful book

SWEET REVENGE

They call me mad, a bitter fool,
but I've been patient, that's my rule.
I stacked your lies, I kept the score,
and built my throne from what you tore.
You thought I'd beg, you thought I'd bleed,
but I was planting every seed.
Years of silence, years of wait,
just to perfect the art of hate.
Now flames are high, your kingdom's through,
and all the world points back to you.
Crazy? Maybe. Cruel? I should.
I did it bad , and it felt so good.

WAY BACK

Love always finds a way back
2 years
No call
Didn't even see you at the mall
We let other people see parts of us that were meant to be ours

One day a sudden urge
Can't get you off my mind
My heart aches like it's missing a piece that I have to find

So slowly I find my way back
To see if ur heart is open, even a crack?
I see u waiting, waiting all along
After seeing the whole world I know it's you to whom I belong
And in coming back to you, I finally come back home

GOOD FOR YOU

The rain is good
It waters the harvest and the wood
But won't it soak me wet if under it I stood

The sweets are good
On a happy occasion I replace them with actual food
But won't it cause me dread if I ate them more than I should

The beach is good
I would sit by the shore all day glued
But it won't hesitate to swallow me if the waters were in a ferocious mood

The people are good
I would have held on to them if I could
But I knew losing myself for love is betraying the girl from my childhood

SCENE OF CRIME

No victim
No killer
But it was a crime scene
All bloody and red and heavy
Heavy with something,
I never wanted to confess
I still think of you with a heaviness in my chest
I still miss you
In moments , in glimpses and in the things you would have said
I still buy you a little gift, from every fest
So if our love was a crime scene
So haunting and maroon
I will confess loud and clear
That It'll always be you

BEST FRIEND

We danced like fools, drinks spilling wide,
Goa nights, barefoot, with the tide.
Sunsets burned pink as we chased the flame,
laughing at the world, shouting each other's name.

Banaras streets, chaos on every lane,
midnight chai, secrets we'd explain.
Manali mornings, wind slicing our hair,
we climbed our fears, screamed truths in the rare air.

We cursed the boyfriends, cursed the ex too,
threw their names in fire, made lies feel untrue.
We've hit the rock bottoms, fallen so low,
felt the cold of the world, its merciless blow.

I held you when darkness swallowed my sight,
you lifted me up, brought me back to the light.
Through heartbreak, through madness, through wild,
reckless nights,
we stitched our girlhood from chaos and fights.

We are fire, we are fury, we are love, we are pain,
we rise from the ruins, we dance in the rain.
my sister, my mirror, my flame,
even in darkness, I'm alive because you came.

EIGHTEEN YEARS, BURNED

Eighteen years, we were roots entwined,
laughing in sunlight, leaving nothing behind.
I trusted you with every secret, every scar,
every tiny fragment of who we are.
And you
you sold it all for him,
for a shadow, a whisper, a hollow whim.
Our childhood, our laughter, our shared mistakes,
all thrown away for the crown you chase.
You wanted praise, the fleeting glow,
so you stepped on me, so you let me go.
I carried our bond like a fragile flame,
and you crushed it, played your hollow game.
Do you remember the nights we cried,
the promises we made, the world we tried?
Or is that gone, a memory burned,
erased by the choice you learned to yearn?
I am fire, I am rage, I am alive,
I survived the knife you used to thrive.
Eighteen years are ashes now,
but I rise from the ruins, I survive,
while you rot in the lie you made your vow.

WALLS OF MY OWN MAKING

I built these walls so high, so tight,
no one could enter, not day nor night.
But now I'm trapped too, lost inside,
a hollow girl with nowhere to hide.
I crave your touch, I crave your fire,
then slam the door on my own desire.
I push, I bite, I scream, I flee,
and curse the chains that live in me.
Love comes near, I let it rot,
I choke on kindness, twist every plot.
I lash at hands that try to hold,
then shiver alone in the freezing cold.
I am the storm that ruins its own,
the queen of ruins, crowned alone.
I built a fortress, now I'm the ghost,
haunting the rooms I wanted most.
I scream at mirrors, I scream at walls,
I scream at the girl behind these halls.
I'm trapped, I'm raging, I'm hollow, I'm bare,
and no one can save me - I don't even dare.

FALL FROM GRACE

I tear myself down with every breath,
a body that whispers, *just wait for death.*
I wear a grin but it doesn't stay,
it cracks, it fades, it rots away.
I call myself names no one will hear,
I bleed out in silence, I choke on fear.
The mirror laughs when I meet its eyes,
spits out my shame, repeats my lies.
I ruin the love, I poison the trust,
I turn what is golden straight into dust.
I push people out, then beg them to stay,
I'm the reason the light keeps slipping away.
I am the venom, the curse, the decay,
the ghost of myself that won't go away.
If hell had a crown, it would rest on my face,
and I'd wear it proud
the fall from grace.

SELF SABOTAGE

I lit the fire,
and then I cursed the smoke.
I broke the glass,
and bled on the shards I broke.
Don't mistake my "sorry" for soft,
it's jagged, it's mean
I'm furious at myself
for killing the best thing I'd seen.
I ran from your love
like it was a crime,
but the truth is I wanted you
all of the time.
I swallowed my fear,
spat it out as lies,
and now it's my own reflection
I can't recognize.
I wasn't heartless
I was reckless,
self-sabotage in a red dress.
And you
you were the one I prayed for,
the one I destroyed,
the one I still ache for.
So hate me,

curse me,
slam every door.
But don't doubt this
I am yours to the core.
I'm sorry,
with rage, with ruin, with flame.
I lost the battle,
but I'll never stop
screaming your name.

FIRSTS AND LASTS OF US

The first time I looked at you
I saw the boy who was sent from above
The first time we kissed
We both felt cosmic love

The last time I looked at you
I saw the boy who I left
The last time we kissed
We both felt our hearts ripping out of our chest

With the last good bye we promised the next time we would do it right and to be better
And the next time we did, just not with each other

GUARDED

My heart is hidden,
with walls built sky-high.
Every heartbreak left me bedridden
now I'm prepared for every goodbye.

It's all bruised,
black, blue, and green.
Each time I felt used,
I wondered if what's good in me
lies beneath my jeans.

My heart is so guarded,
so move with gentle grace.
See my soul
not just my face.
Let me rest in your tender embrace,
and if I let you in,
know it's an exceptional case.

I flinched at first
not because I didn't care,
but because I've learned
to be scared.
You didn't force your way in,

you waited.
Held space for the quiet,
for the parts I never translated.

You didn't break down walls
you gently knocked,
and waited for me
to unlock.
Because once you were in,
it wasn't just some empty space
you filled it with warmth,
and made it feel like a place
that finally felt safe.

FINAL ACT OF LOVE

They all say
The final act of love is letting you go
I held u for too long
Drowned you with my love song
Apologised even when you were in the wrong
For what?
Just so to each other we belong

So I'm sorry
For calling
For begging
For crying
For screaming
For promising to never give up
I release you
And I release me

As my final act of love
I'll let u fly out like dove
No more cages of memories tight,
No more holding on through the night.

May the winds be kind as you drift away,
And may peace find me, come what may.

I'll fold away the "what if's and "why"s,
And meet the sunrise with open eyes.

Not all love is meant to stay,
Some teach us how to walk away.
But loving you
Was never in vain.
Even in loss, something sweet will remain.

So I'll walk ahead, no backward glance,
Give time and heart a second chance.
For love, real love, must set things free
And in freeing you,
I come back to me

TROPHY

She is wanted by all
Needed by none
After many trials
Finally won by the number one

He keeps her covered in diamonds
She is placed in glass trunk
He shows her off
While everyone claps
The poor trophy thinks it's her
But it's for the man that won

The cheap metal and the dark emptiness
Hidden by the diamonds is seen by none
The trophy sits alone
The light can't get inside
How can it surpass the diamonds that bring her so much pride
She sits empty and dark in her dome

Till one day her diamonds fall off
The cheap metal and rust
Makes him full of disgust
So he replaces her

With a new one covered in gold dust
When everyone claps again
The new trophy thinks it her
Oh lord the poor girl, it not you it's for your conquerer

RAIN

When I meet the one
Please let it be on a day it'll rain
Let it all come pouring down
Like The answer to why I had to go through all of that pain
The glistening leaves
Will match my shining eyes that are in love simple and plain
Let us be soaking wet
And dance under it like we are insane
Let the winds blow so fast
That all I hear is the beating of my heart and no thoughts of my brain
Let the rain be a sign
That this love will set me free from everything that held me down with chain

MEANT FOR YOU

They say , what's meant for you will always find you
And I hope that's true
I let you go
You did the same
No where to be found
Was this a game?
But I guess universe has its own way
So when I go to pray
You are standing right next to me on a Tuesday
Our eyes lock for a seconds few
And just like that I see a glimpse of me and you

ALL MY GHOSTS

As I blow out all candles on my cake
1,2,3,4.........20
20?
As I close my eyes for a wish I have to make

I see a little girl only three
Tangled hair and Bare feet
She laughed so loud perhaps for she was free

I see a girl not mare than thirteen
Hating her body
Her head down in front of everyone who was mean

I see a girl who was once seventeen
Falling in love
She thought love was like a beautiful dream

I see girl who is nineteen
Lost, beaten down and afraid
All she wanted was to be seen

As I blow out the last candle
I think about the girl I have become
To define her will be a very risky gamble

She loves her freedom
She who has fallen down is not a damsel
She rose above her demons to build her own kingdom

YOU ARE SORRY- A CONSPIRACY THEORY

I have a theory in my head
you still think about me before going to bed
If we ever had a last conversation what would you have said
It's like a letter in my mind left unread
You are sorry and it causes you dread
Thousands of tears you have shed
But here I am laying in my bed
There is no way to know because after all it's just a conspiracy theory in my head

WRITE

I write so frantically
Till the point I can't breathe
The idea consumes me so gigantically
That I write the words that can't come out of my shivering teeth

TRUE LOVE'S KISS

So kiss me today and every day
Till the days turn into nights
The sloppy disgusting kisses
The kisses where we stop and look into each others eyes
Kiss me like you've never kissed anyone
Kiss me like you mean it
Kiss me good night
And Kiss me when we fight
Kiss me like you want me with every cell and bone
Kiss me like the world is ending and you'd still rather be by my side
Kiss me when I am wide awake and kiss me when I am asleep
Kiss me till the day I realise that there are no kisses left for me to seek

AIRPLANE

I'll be like an airplane
I looked at her in surprise, Wondering is she even sane
Yes you heard me right
Questioning eyes full of disdain
She smiled at me and said it again,
It carries so much baggage yet it flies
It still stays in its lane
And eventually it reach's it's destination
Aren't we all airplanes I wondered
With baggage stored in our bodies and mind,
We must carry it for our life, it's a part of us and we can't leave it behind ,
But will I reach the destination ? I wonder on the days when my navigation skills are at loss
The days when fuel is running so low like the little packet of sauce
The days with turbulent weather and I can't see across
I don't know what and where my destination is so somedays I just take a toss
yet it was a little easier a little clearer with u by my side
My copilot helping my with all the lefts and rights
I guess I'll still figure it out, your stop has come, but it's my plane at the end of the night

HURT

Hurt they say is a simple four letter word
Love they say is a simple four letter word
When love ends it is replaced by hurt
It fills the void perfectly
Both take up the same space after all , four letters
I scream on the top of my lungs
I cry till I can't breathe anymore
My skin is slit up with blood pouring out just so I can feel something more than hurt
my heart is pounding and my face is red and puffy with all the tears i have cried
All the sleepless nights
All of this for what I wonder
Love makes me feel alive
Love makes me smile
Love gives me a reason to be
Love is my muse
But afterall Love is just the shade of an ivy tree in the summer afternoon
Love and hurt go together, hand in hand as if they both are rulers of the same land
Love they say is a simple four letter word replaced by hurt when it ends

INTIMACY

I have walked along a million feet
I have laid my head on a thousand shoulders
I have held a hundred hands
I have kissed a dozen lips
I have fallen in love with two
But I had never experienced intimacy true
Until our foreheads touched and I looked so deeply into his eyes
We were bare with no disguise
Before we could blink twice
This was true intimacy I realised
Because without him saying a word I understood the reason behind all his painful cries
The hurt in his heart never scared me, it left me mesmerised

DISTANCE

There is a selfishness in distance
The pain of it is present in our existence
the happiness of it is hidden
I don't want my fondness for you to be erased and rewritten
For I can't love someone I don't know
To save my beloved, I'll let you go
So when I walk by trying not to look
It's simply so that our chapter still stays my favourite in the book

HIS AND HER

His hands are as callous as the rugged mat
Her hands are as soft as furry cat
His jaws are sharp as bows
Her face as tender as rose
His voice is as ferocious as the storm
Her voice is as delicate as a new born

The his and her make me wonder
Her must be feeble
But his can be hurt by a single needle
As her watches him go
She realises there is nothing as frail as his ego

WRITE ME A SONG

I make you immortal with ink on paper
I'll write about how I love your crooked nose
How when we snuggle there is tingling of our toes
I'll write you a poem I'll write you a prose
I'll write about the pain that grows
I know you are no writer or a raper
I don't ask much
But can make me immortal with your paint brush
Can you write me a song
With all the rights and no wrong
A song about us
I won't care if it's the worse
The tune will be our laugh
The verses will be about how I am your better half
The lyrics are my favourite part
They will be about love written with a broken heart

RECIPE FOR DISASTER

We begin by boiling some water on excessive heat
We add some thyme , need more of it but no one has it on the streets
We add some chilli's, some should be enough to burn our hearts and wet our eyes
But I add more of it for the pain they cause then I can hear loud cries
I add some chicken hearts
Best served when chopped into tiny pieces
Add a vegetable grown from the drop a blood
It's not sinful to me
For the rulers and rich drink chilled blood as a welcome drink
I mix it all it's well combined to give it to humanity who thrives in envy
But as I get out there are scavengers, who should I serve when there are so many

DARK

As a kid I was scared of the dark
As the lights turned off
I was afraid of the monsters under my bed
I know about these monsters from the stories I've read

As I grew up I lived in the dark
Afraid of a spark
The darkness ties my existence with a thread
I despise the spark for it will never spread
Causing me nothing except dread

The monsters are no longer under my bed
No, they're not dead
They've crept up and now live in my head

MAD WOMAN IN THE ATTIC

Confined within the four walls
For they are afraid of me
Accused with allegations that are false
Intimidated by my individuality, if I were to be free

I am Bertha Mason and every other women
Punished by the society for not being enough
If I leave my kitchen I am driven to the prison
I am the exile I am the villain
It's my life yet who I will be is their decision
It's not just my story it is a tale of millions

LEARNING

I've learnt the importance of friendship
From my closet friends
I've learnt the importance of family
From my mom and dad
I've learnt the importance of love
From a dead love letter
I've learnt hate
From the blade against my skin
I've learnt to appreciate all except myself
From the society and values I was brought up with
I've learnt to love myself, truly, fully and exceptionally
From all the disappointments

MUSE

My muse is not love
My muse is not hate
My muse is not the people who walk away
My muse is not peace
My muse is not chaos
My muse is not war
My muse is not victory
What should my my muse be I wonder casually

My muse is agony
My muse is tragedy
My muse speaks frantically
My muse exists in fantasy
If you can't guess it still, my muse is my insanity

IRONY

Cold of January only makes me miss the warmth of july
We only meet people to say goodbye
Our graves dug deep after overdose to experience the high
Words coming out of our mouth are subject to lies, but we trust the verity of the eyes
The letters we don't throw even when the meaning of words in it dies
That's the irony of life giving us hope only so that the possibility of it could be denied

POETS AND MEDUSA

In the beginning both are heavenly
Both exist like ebony
Both have committed a felony
The middle is full of rage
A wickedness that can't be cleansed with the holy sage
Their names mentioned in books page after page
The end is brutal
Their suffering and grief met with disapproval
They are subject to retribution, making them the villains who were so cruel
In death they rise
There words of vengeance heard from the skies
Heard by all but understood by the wise
Are they really villains or victims in disguise ?

LOST

As I grow up
I tend to lose a lot
Friendship once held so close to the heart
Love so dear is falling apart
Ever consuming thoughts turned into art
The grades that validated me being smart

As I lose people and feelings
I am left bleeding
Only to be dawned with a realisation
All the opinions about me should be consumed with some filtration
So I am happy to lose the ones that are a barrier
Ones that make my nights dark rather than starrier

SILENCE

The room is silent
My mind is not
The sulking of my heart
Turned into art
For my pen screams so loud
That even the silence has bowed

FORGIVE

I forgive you so I can forgive myself
To burn all the hate and guilt stored in my heart's shelf
Love hate and indifference
Just three phases engulfing my whole existence
Have to sit with my thoughts for my soul's independence
To come out of it there can be no ignorance
Love is a gamble
Hate a vicious seed

Letting go the idea of being saved by someone, I am no damsel in need
Before indifference comes
There is a constant war between love and hate
Not just for the once upon a time dream but even for my own self indeed
Day after day the back and forth movement fills me up
Till I finally decide to empty the cup
For this requires to forgive you and I both
Repentance for the sins
To let go of the good I also let go of the bad
And I forgive you first for driving me mad
Then I forgive me for disrespecting myself to save what we once had

GUILT

It's an ever consuming feeling
I lay in my bed all day long starting at the ceiling
An amalgamation of emotions suppressed because ;
anxiety consumes me when with them I am dealing
My coat of strength that I hide under is peeling
The inside is dark dreary and freezing
I am afraid of the demons inside me and which one
will I be meeting
The thoughts of hurt and pain is on what they're
feeding
The good inside my heart has somehow stopped
believing
I feel like crying and screaming
Guilt you see is an ever consuming feeling
Making me wonder if I was ever even healing

DAD

I have heard people talk about their dad
In words that are often bad
My dad on the other hand is not like them making me feel glad

He Always has my back
Fills up the drawers with my favourite snacks
Not to brag but
He is the the best dad with nothing to lack

He pushes me to be my best
Talks to me when I am feeling stressed
Showed me what love is like in all the five languages
Holding my hand even through the darkest passages

REALITY

My opinions might be subject to partiality
But it's a bore when I live only in reality
The world of ink offers immortality
Words fill my imagination's cavity
Sitting in my room i meet people of a different locality
Sweeping me in a world far away from the earth's gravity

SOUL

Believe it or not it's centuries old
Body can perish but the soul never grows cold
The habits and traumas of my past life it holds
A man can be bought but his soul never sold

SKIN AND BONES

They are all that's left
A body full of warmth lost in the quest for the best
Numbers on the scale making me obsessed
Measuring my waist and chest
Why can't I fit into that vest
It drives me crazy leaving me distressed
Beauty standards determined by The ideal's of the west
Why can't I fit into those even though I try my best
Living in a world where a woman's worth is dictated by how well she is dressed
It's my own body then why do I feel like a guest
It's not beauty anymore it's an open theft

TACOS

Chilli's-crispy chicken tacos for two
Turned into I don't even recognise you
three tacos sometimes a cold brew
Turned into all we do is argue
Tacos, holding us together like a glue
Turned into was any of even true

SERIOUSNESS OF LIFE

I've learnt to let it slip
People come and people go
Nothing here forever sticks
It's amalgamation of random things
A day of happiness and the other of despair
All days will pass soon
Leaving memories for us to share
So seriousness of life, I've learnt to let it go
Laughing all the way because what is life? No one knows

LAYERS

I wonder when I was born who was I meant to be
For all the people i have met add a new layer to me
These layers weigh me down
And uplift me to be a perfect construct society wants to see
I lay under it hidden somewhere only to be found in dreams
A snail in its shell
It's a part of me
Under all these layers will I find the real me?

SUNFLOWER

In a field of roses
Lovers that come to capture the beauty are stung by the thorns
Thorns hidden under the luscious petals that the heart desires
Is a threat of enchanting beauty leading us to a path which will set our existence on fire
I keep my head down at nights for there is no sun to uplift me when the lovers hour is struck
No thorns on my stems to protect me
For I am not desired
Not professed love to
For I rise and bloom when the dawn is struck
In a field of roses I am a sunflower
Not scared to be plucked
Yet waiting in anticipation wondering if I'll ever find love even if it's by sheer luck

POSSIBILITY OF A DREAM

Dreams?
Not a reality or a reality yet to be created
Dreams and reality there is just a fine line
Money plants turning into money trees
Deleted drafts turning into diary read till dawn
Possibility of a dream I wonder could it ever come true
Or is the idea too obscene

I LOVE YOU

I love the way you make me smile
I love the way you make life worth its while
I love way you hold my hand
I love the way you play with my hair strand
I love the way that all you do now is irritate
I love way your words were baneful so I can suffocate
I love the way you made me feel like it was a mistake
I love the way you betrayed
But most of all I love the way you lie about love when all you do is just tolerate
I love you so much that I can't differentiate
What is love and what is hate?

I KILLED WHO I USED TO BE

She who loved so hard
And was left scared
She who trusted so easy
And was left feeling crazy
She who was so kind
And was left thinking she had no mind
So I killed all the parts that led me to ruin
I was no cinderella so I kept my shoes in
I lost what made me humane
I lost her and turned into a stone
But I finally belonged to a self that was my own
I had my own voice with a certainty in my tone
I created my reality and sat on the throne
I killed the vulnerable me who was scared to be alone
I lost her to be a girl who is strong

CRY

As my heart grows colder it shifts it's warmth across my cheeks
Somedays it burns red with anguish I can't explain
Somedays my eyes are glistening with salty yet warm pearls
The warmth of my heart is stolen by the forces of this world
Friends, family and the love that I once held so close
All have left at a gentle pace
It's a destitute place
Cold and barren
All it's warmth shifted to anger and anguish and slowly shed off with glistening pearls dried up with the warmth my heart once held

LET THEM

I stay quiet and let them
I let them jerk themselves off while touching my thighs
Oh it's my fault, wearing a skirt making their sexual drive to arise
So I stay quiet because oh what a girl is if not nice
So i let them hit me
Hit me hard that it haunts me to this night
Oh it's my fault, for no matter how hard I tried I was not a student who was bright
So I stay quiet because oh she my mom and we can't fight
So I let them laugh at me
You're legs have hair! Are you a he or a she?
Oh it's my fault, for feeling comfortable in my skin, you see
So I stay quiet because what is a girl if has choices that are free
So I let them exploit my virtue
Make love to me because oh I loved you so and believed for it to be true
Oh it's my fault, you're a man , just a man nothing new
So I stay quiet, because maybe I am just something you used and threw

So I let them dictate my worth
In a society where my role is just to serve
Oh it's my fault, Simply because I am a women by birth
So I stay quiet, because it's a generational curse

HAIR

Hair they say hold memories and grief
Yet we adorn it with the most beautiful leaves
It's a symbol of beauty for all the ladies
Its comes at varying lengths short to as long as touching the knees
It moves gently when comes face to face with breeze
Yet I believe
Hair is just a piece of the true beauty that lies underneath
A shaved head in fact i wonder would give me such a relief
From all the hassles of a combs teeth
And more importantly from all the memories and grief

JUST A GLANCE

I took in his lips
The way they crashed against mine
It felt like the universe sung for me,
The illusion of fate and destiny
Must have been true for you and me,
I was floating up high
My mind had never been so free ,
I was always yours, how could it not be,
Until I realised
That it was just a glance
And in my mind were all, phantom stories

THE LAST TIME I LEAVE

I zip the bag too quickly,
as if speed will keep the memories
from spilling out.
The room is still
curtains breathing,
walls holding every word
we threw like stones,
every promise that cracked
before it ever lived.

My hands linger on the doorframe.
I almost want the walls to beg me to stay,
but they've grown used to watching me go.

The lies are folded neatly in the suitcase,
the broken friendships tucked in corners,
the loves that burned out too soon
pressed flat between shirts.

I don't slam the door.
I close it softly,
because even goodbyes deserve gentleness.

The hurt follows me,
but so does the air
new, sharp, endless.

Leaving doesn't heal me.
It doesn't fix what's broken.
It only gives me silence enough
to breathe without breaking.

And maybe that is all I need tonight
to walk away,
to be the girl who disappears
before the storm swallows her whole.